How do I u...

Key Words with ...
parallel series, each ...
series are written usin...
vocabulary. Readers will get the most out of **Key Wo...** with
Peter and Jane when they follow the books in the pattern
1a, 1b, 1c; 2a, 2b, 2c and so on.

• Series a

gradually introduces and repeats new words.

• Series b

provides further practice of these same words, but
in a different context and with different illustrations.

• Series c

uses familiar words to teach **phonics** in a methodical way,
enabling children to read increasingly difficult words.
It also provides a link to writing.

Published by Ladybird Books Ltd
A Penguin Company
Penguin Books Ltd., 80 Strand, London WC2R 0RL, UK
Penguin Books Australia Ltd, 707 Collins Street, Melbourne, Victoria 3008, Australia
Penguin Group (NZ) 67 Apollo Drive, Rosedale, North Shore 0632, New Zealand

019

ISBN: 978-1-40930-147-9

Printed in China

Key Words

with Peter and Jane

10b Adventure at the castle

written by W. Murray
illustrated by J.H. Wingfield

As John and Simon got ready for their holiday they talked to each other of what they hoped to see and do. They both wanted to drive a long way to see places that were new to them. They also wanted to camp, to bathe and to fish. Their mother let them have her car for their holiday and helped them to decide what food to take. They put this in a box in the back of the car. Most of the food was in tins. They would be able to buy other food on the way.

They put their telescope and fishing rods inside the car. Then they tied the tent on to the top of the car.

"I hope we have some fine weather," said John. "It won't be much fun if it rains all the time. We ought to take some books to read."

"Yes," said Simon, "we will take some books, but let's hope for the best with the weather."

They went inside the house to tell their mother and father that they were ready to leave. Then they got into the car and were soon on their way. It was John's turn to drive.

John drove a long way and then he let Simon drive the car. The two brothers did not drive too fast.

When they were tired they stopped to make a camp for the night. They asked a farmer if they could put their tent near one of his large barns for the night.

"Yes, of course you may," he said. "I liked to camp when I was a boy." They talked to the farmer about their holiday. Then they had something to eat and went to bed.

"I hope we sleep well," said Simon to John. "I am sure we will because we are tired," said his brother. They did sleep well, all the night through.

In the morning they got up, washed, and had their breakfast. They thanked the farmer and drove off with their tent on top of their car.

"The car runs well, doesn't it?" said Simon. "Yes," answered John, "but I do hope the engine doesn't go wrong." "There you go again," laughed Simon. "Don't worry, I am sure the engine won't go wrong."

When they came to a town new to them, they stopped the car and got out to have a look round.

The next night, the boys made their camp by a river. They found a beautiful place on the river bank, with green grass and some lovely trees. During the first day there was plenty of work to do to get the camp ready for their use. Then they had time to bathe and fish. They did not put the tent too near the river bank. It is not safe to camp too near water.

Some way ahead, at a bend in the river, they could see a castle. It looked a very interesting place.

"Does the river flow from us to the castle or from the castle to us?" John asked Simon. "It flows from the castle to us," said Simon. "The water comes from the hills behind the castle and flows past the castle and past us on its way to the sea."

"The castle looks very old," said John. "Do you think anyone lives there? If not we might be able to explore it."

Simon said, "We can't tell from here if anyone lives in the castle or not, but we could easily find out if we went there. It would be fun to explore it."

John sat on the bank of the river and fished while Simon made a raft. "Why are you making that raft?" John asked his brother.

"I want to fish further out from the bank," answered Simon. "There may be some big fish further out in the river. Also I think it is fun to have a raft. We might use it when we bathe."

Before long, Simon put his raft on the water and climbed on to it. He had made two paddles as well as the raft. He soon found that his raft moved downstream quite quickly. As he did not want the raft to move along in the water, he got a rock and tied a rope to it. Then he let the heavy rock down into the water by the rope until it was on the river bed. He tied the other end of the rope to the raft so that it stayed in the same place while the water flowed by.

Then Simon fished. Soon he had some fish on the raft. A few were quite large.

John had stopped fishing. He was looking up-stream towards the castle at the bend in the river.

"Look at the castle," called out John to his brother. "Do you see what I see? I'm sure a light is shining from the wall."

Simon looked towards the castle. "No," he said, "I can't see anything." Then he said, "Wait a minute. Yes, I can. There is a light flashing from the castle wall."

"Someone is using a mirror to flash the light from the sun," said John. "He seems to be flashing it at us. There it goes again."

"It could be a boy or girl at play," said Simon, "or it could be someone who wants us to give him help. How can we find out?" He paddled his raft to the bank where John sat.

The two boys talked together for a few minutes and then John said, "I'll get the telescope. We'll be able to see more with that."

He was soon looking through the telescope towards the castle. "I can see a boy about nine or ten years old behind the outside wall of the castle," he said. "He is flashing a mirror at us." Then he gave the telescope to his brother.

"Yes," said Simon. "I can see the young boy now."

Simon and John decided to drive to the castle. They wanted to talk to the boy they had seen flashing the mirror at them.

They put away their telescope and got into their car. Then they drove off towards the castle to try to see the boy. A road ran close to the river bank nearly all the way. When they got to the castle they found that there was water all round it. The castle was an island in the river. They drove their car close to the edge of the river and got out. There was no way across the water into the castle.

There was a drawbridge but it had been pulled up. "If someone let down that drawbridge we could get across the water into the castle," said John. "Let's call out until someone comes."

They called across to the castle and then waited. Nobody came. Nobody let down the drawbridge. They called out again but nothing happened. Once more they called out and waited. However, there was no answer.

"I'm afraid nobody is going to answer. We must go now," said Simon. The boys turned their car around and drove away to their camp.

When they got back to their camp, Simon and John saw through the telescope that the boy had gone from the wall.

The next morning, they could see him there again. However, he did not flash his mirror at the boys. He seemed to be doing something with some bottles. Every now and again he would throw one over the castle wall into the river.

"Do you think the boy is playing a game?" John asked his brother. "I don't know," answered Simon. "It seems to me that he puts something into each bottle before he throws it into the river. Why should he do that?"

"It seems funny to me," said John. "He seems to write on a piece of paper, then put the paper into a bottle and throw it over the wall."

"The bottles will be coming down the river past our camp," said Simon. "Let's get on the raft and catch some of the bottles, then we can see what is inside. The boy may be sending us a message. We can read the writing on the paper inside the bottles."

John and Simon put their raft on the water and looked for some of the bottles they had seen the boy throw from the castle. For some time they could not see anything like a bottle in the water.

"We must find one," said Simon. "I feel sure that the boy has sent us a message."

"There's one!" called out John. "There's a bottle going along slowly by the other bank!"

The boys paddled the raft across the river until Simon could take the bottle out of the water. It was not damaged, and the paper inside it was dry. Simon got out the paper, looked at it, and said, "Yes, it is a message. It says, 'Please help. I am alone in the castle with my uncle who is very ill. I can't work the drawbridge.'

Philip Jones."

"I am glad we have found the message," said John. "We must help the boy at once. We must get a doctor to see his uncle."

"Yes," said Simon, "but how can we get the uncle to a doctor, or a doctor to come to the uncle, if we can't get the drawbridge down? We must think of a way to get into the castle."

"Think hard," said John. "We must find a way into the castle as quickly as possible."

"There is a policeman's house not far away," said Simon. "Let's go there for help."

The two boys went by car to call on the policeman, but they found that he was out. He would not be back until the afternoon. Then they decided to go by raft up to the castle wall to try to talk to the boy.

They paddled the raft up to the castle wall. They could see the boy's head as he looked down on them from the top. Simon called up to the boy. "Have you a rope? If so, tie one end up there and throw the other end down to us."

The boy went away. He soon came back with a light rope which he let down to the raft. Simon pulled at it. "It isn't very strong," he said. "I may be too heavy for this rope, but I'll try it." He started to climb up towards the top of the wall. John waited below on the raft. "This is exciting," he said to himself.

Suddenly the rope broke and Simon fell heavily into the water by the raft.

One minute Simon was climbing up the rope, and the next he was swimming in the cold water of the river.

"What happened?" called the boy from the top of the wall. "The rope broke suddenly," said John. "My brother is in the water. "It's all right, he is a good swimmer and he will be safe."

Simon soon climbed over the side of the raft. "Have a rest while we think what to do next," said John.

"Don't go away," called the boy. "I have a heavy rope. I will go and get it." He soon came back with a heavy rope which he let down to the raft.

Although he was wet through, Simon again started to climb to the top of the wall. In a few minutes he was with the boy at the top. Then John climbed up. "I have tied the rope to the raft," he said.

"Let me take you to my uncle," said Philip. "Please come with me."

He talked as they went along. "We have a fire and you will soon get dry by it. My uncle is asleep but he will be able to talk to you when he wakes up."

"My uncle lives alone in this castle although he is getting old," said Philip. "I am here on holiday. My mother and father are coming to take me home in a week's time."

"How long has your uncle been ill?" asked Simon. "He has been ill for two days," answered Philip. "There is no telephone and the drawbridge has gone wrong. I can't make it work at all."

"We will have a look at it in a minute," said John. "We ought to see your uncle first, though." "Yes," said Philip. "Here is his room." They went in to stand by the bed. Philip's uncle was asleep. "We should not wake him," said Simon. "Let me get dry by your fire and then take us to the drawbridge."

The two boys tried to make the drawbridge work as it should, but they were not able to do so. Then they went back to Philip's uncle to find that he was awake. He was glad to see them and asked if they could bring a doctor to him. "Yes, of course," said Simon. "Don't worry. We will go for a doctor. He will soon be here to see you."

The two brothers left Philip at the castle to look after his uncle while they went off to get help. They climbed down the rope to the raft and paddled down the river to their camp. Here they got into the car and set off to find the policeman and a doctor.

They were in luck. When they got to his house, the policeman had just come home. He was having a busy day. He had some tea and biscuits as they told him what they had found at the castle.

"The boy's uncle wants help badly," said Simon. "But first we must be able to let the drawbridge down."

"I will bring some tools to mend the drawbridge," said the policeman. "We can go up the river in my boat and climb up the rope into the castle. I will telephone the doctor now and ask him to go by ambulance and wait for us to let the drawbridge down."

When he had telephoned the doctor they went with the policeman to the river. His boat was tied to a buoy by the bridge. They all got into the boat and were soon moving upstream towards the castle.

The policeman said, "I know Mr. Jones, the boy's uncle. He is a rich man who has lived alone at the castle for nine or ten years. He is getting too old to live alone now. I have told him many times that he ought to have a telephone at the castle. I am sure he will have one put in after this."

John, Simon and the policeman climbed in turn up the rope to the top of the castle wall. Philip was waiting there. He was glad to see them, and quickly took them down to see his uncle.

"The doctor is on his way," said the policeman to Mr. Jones. "Don't worry, we'll look after you and Philip here. We are just going to mend the drawbridge so that the doctor can come in to see you."

Simon and the policeman went down to the drawbridge. They were able to mend it, using the tools the policeman had brought. Then they let down the drawbridge for the doctor. The ambulance waited outside.

After the doctor had seen Mr. Jones he said that he should be taken to the hospital at once. He went with him in the ambulance.

The policeman set off home in his boat.

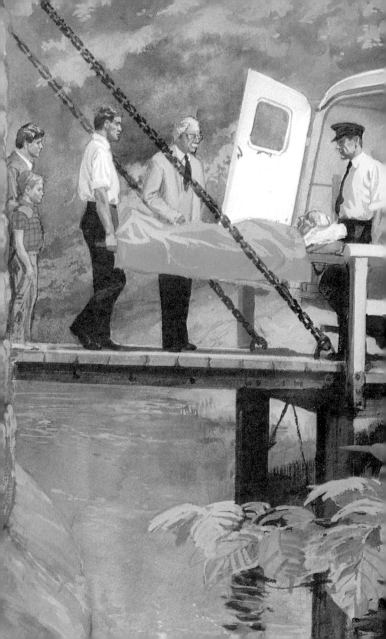

Before he left for the hospital, Mr. Jones asked the two brothers to stay with Philip at the castle for a week. Then Philip's mother and father would come to take him home. The two boys said that they would be happy to do this.

Soon after the ambulance left, a storm started. The rain came down heavily and there was thunder and lightning. Philip said, "I don't like to be alone during storms, and they keep me awake at night. I would be afraid if you were not here with me."

John told Philip that he and his brother had had an adventure in a storm when they were on an island with their two cousins. The young boy asked John to tell him about it.

"We went to an island to bathe and explore," said John, "and when we were there a storm smashed our little boat on the beach. It also damaged the engine of our motor boat which we had tied to a buoy. The motor boat was too big to row back to the mainland. All we could do was to send up a rocket at night. Our father wasn't long getting across to us in another boat."

The storm did not last long and the three boys had a good night's sleep. In the morning, they left the castle to go to the hospital. They wanted to know how Philip's uncle was, and were very glad to find that he was getting well again. However, he had been told that he would have to stay in hospital for about two weeks.

Mr. Jones told Simon and John that he had lived alone too long, and that when he went back to the castle he was going to have a friend to live with him. He asked the brothers if they would arrange for a telephone to be fitted at the castle and for a television set to be fitted as well.

Simon said that they would be happy to arrange for both a telephone and a television set to be put in. Then they asked Mr. Jones if they could explore the castle.

"Yes," he said. "You will find it an interesting place." He told them that a room in his castle had a secret cupboard and that they could find and open this secret cupboard. "It was used to hide people in years gone by," he said.

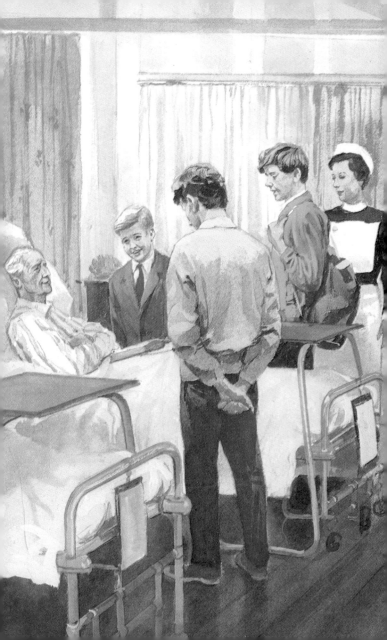

The boys found it interesting to watch the men as they fitted the television set. When they all went up on the roof of the castle, the three boys used their telescope to look around. They could see a long way from the roof as they were so far up, as the telescope was a good one. They could see the sea, and Simon said he could just see the rocks on the shore. "I didn't know that we were so close to the sea," he said. "We could drive over there one day, to bathe."

"We must go there soon," said John. "It is beautiful weather for a swim, but we can't go this afternoon as the men are coming to put in the telephone."

They were glad when the men had come with the telephone. Philip used it first and talked to the nurse at the hospital about his uncle. She told him that Mr. Jones had just had some soup and was to get out of bed for a little while that day.

Simon then telephoned the policeman. He thanked him very much for his help on the day when Mr. Jones went to hospital.

"Now we can explore the castle," said Simon to John and Philip. "Let's start on the top floor." The three kept together as they looked into every room. There was much of interest to see. Mr. Jones was a rich man. For many years he had collected pictures, photographs, old guns, tools and other interesting things. The boys liked the guns best.

They looked for some time at a photograph, taken from an aeroplane, of the castle and the woods around it. "Uncle owns all this," said Philip. "Part of the river is his, as well."

"Do you know about the secret cupboard?" Simon asked Philip. "Your uncle told us how to find it." "No," said Philip. "I know nothing about the secret cupboard, but I would like to see it. Did Uncle tell you if he keeps anything in it?"

"I don't think there is anything in it," said Simon. "It is a big cupboard. A man could hide in it. Mr. Jones said it was used to hide people many years ago. "Come on," said Philip. "Let's find the secret cupboard now and get in it. That would be exciting. I can't wait to see it."

They went to explore the last room. "It gets more exciting now," said John, "because this is the room with the secret cupboard."

"Yes, this is the one," said Simon. "Here are the panels Mr. Jones told us about. That must be the wall, and there is the mark. He said that the panel we had to move would have a mark on it. We ought to be able to push the panel along."

"It becomes more exciting every minute," said Philip. "Let me help." Simon and Philip both tried to push the panel along but nothing happened.

"It isn't moving," said John. "Here, let me help." He helped the others to try to push the wood along, but again nothing happened.

"Wait a minute," said Simon. "Stop! Let's push the other way." They pushed the panel the other way and it moved along easily.

"Look at that!" called out Philip. "There it is! There's the secret cupboard! Push it along further so that I can get in."

"Wait a minute," said Simon. "Let's have a look first. We want to make sure it's safe."

When the panel was pushed right back, the boys looked into the secret cupboard. "It is big," said Simon. "It's more like a little room than a cupboard. It looks safe to me. I will get in first." He climbed into the cupboard while the others watched. Then he got out, and John and Philip climbed in.

"There is nothing in here," said John, "and it would be dark if you closed the panel. Close it now." Simon closed the panel of the secret cupboard for a minute. Then he opened it again. John and Philip got out.

Simon looked at the floor of the cupboard. "Look at this," he said. "Can you see what I see?" "I can't see anything," said Philip, but John said, "I think I see a trapdoor in the floor of the cupboard."

"Yes, so do I," said Simon. "Mr. Jones didn't say anything about a trap-door. He told me about the cupboard and nothing else." Simon climbed again into the cupboard to have a close look at the floor.

"Open it!" said John. "Open the trap-door, Simon. Open it and look down." "I don't know if I can," answered his brother. "I will try."

After a few minutes Simon got the trap-door open. He looked down but could see nothing as it was so dark. "We must have a light," he said.

John handed a lamp to his brother. Then Simon said, "There are steps down to a little room. I think I'll go down." As Simon went down the steps, John climbed into the cupboard. Then he went down the steps after his brother. Philip stayed at the top. By the light of the lamp the two brothers could see that they were in a little room with no door or windows. There was nothing in the room but one large box.

John tried to open the box but it was locked. Then he tried to move it, and found that it was not heavy. Simon said, "I don't think we should move the box or open it until we have asked Mr. Jones. Do you think he knows about this little room? It seems funny to me that he didn't tell us about it."

"Let's go and see Mr. Jones," said John. "We will tell him about the room and the box. He may let us open the box."

The three boys went to the hospital again to see Mr. Jones. It was the day after they had found the secret room. First they told Mr. Jones about the television and the telephone. He was very pleased to hear that both these had been put into the castle. "I am so glad you have taken an interest in these things for me," he said. "I must give you a present for helping me."

Then they told him that they had found the secret cupboard. "You didn't tell us about the secret room, though," said Simon. "A secret room?" asked Mr. Jones.

The boys told him that they had found a trap-door in the floor of the secret cupboard, and some steps which went down to a small room without doors or windows. "I know nothing of this," said Mr. Jones. "Is there anything in the room?" Simon answered. "Only a box," he said, "and it is locked."

"I would like you to open the box for me," said Uncle. "I have a lot of old keys at the castle. You could try some of these to open the lock. Please bring me what you find inside the box."

When they got back to the castle, the boys tried to find a key to unlock the box. Mr. Jones had told them where to find the old keys. Many of these were much too big for the lock on the box and others were too small. It was some time before Simon said, "I think this is the one we want. This will do it." He turned the key and at last the box was unlocked.

All three were excited as Simon opened the box. John had one quick look and said, "Papers, just papers!" "Yes," said Philip, "only old papers. Those are not very exciting!"

"We don't know," said Simon. "They may be very interesting. They may be valuable." He took a close look at some of the papers. "They are hard to read," he said. "The writing is very old. They seem to be about the castle and the people who lived here many years ago. Mr. Jones will find them interesting."

"Take all the papers out," said John. "There may be something else in the box." Simon put all the papers on the table and John said, "There is something else! Is that a small leather bag?"

There was a little leather bag in the box. John took the bag, opened it and looked inside. "There are some rings and coins in here," he said. He put them on the table. There were four rings and six coins. Simon said, "They may be valuable. They look as if they are very old and made of gold. We must take them to Mr. Jones."

At the hospital, they found Mr. Jones out in the sun looking very well. When he saw them he said, "I feel happy. The doctor is pleased with me and he says that I may go home in a few days. Did you open the box?"

"Yes," said Simon. "We have brought the things we found in it. Here are some old papers and a little leather bag."

Mr. Jones read some of the papers. "It becomes interesting," he said, "very, very interesting. These tell me some of the things I wanted to know about my castle." Then he opened the leather bag and took a close look at the rings and coins. "Some are gold," he said. "You three boys may have the coins for helping me. There are two for each of you."

The boys talked about their coins on the way back to the castle. "Mr. Jones says that we may do as we like with the coins," said John. "We could sell them when we get home, Simon." "Yes," answered his brother, "I think we could sell the gold ones for quite a lot of money."

At the castle Philip found a letter from his mother and father. He read it and then said to John and Simon, "My mother and father write to say that their holiday is over and that they are on their way to the castle to take me home."

Mr. and Mrs. Jones drove up to the castle during the afternoon of the next day. Mr. Jones did not know that his brother, Philip's uncle, had been taken ill. When Philip told them, Mr. and Mrs. Jones went to the hospital at once. When they came back to the castle, they thanked Simon and John for the help they had given. Then Philip got into their car and they drove off.

Simon and John stayed on at the castle until Mr. Jones came back from hospital to live at the castle with a friend.

New words used in this book

Total number of new words: 54